NIG___
My Iditarod Adventure

STORY BY NANCY YOSHIDA
ILLUSTRATIONS BY JON VAN ZYLE

REACH FOR THE SKY PUBLISHING
THOMPSON ND

© Copyright 2011 by Nancy Yoshida
TXU 1-764-352

All rights reserved. No part of this book or artwork, may be reproduced or utilized in any form or by any means, electronic or mechanical, including photocopying, recording, or by any information storage or retrieval system, without permission in writing from the Publisher or artist.

Submit to: Publisher, Reach for the Sky Publishing
1079 Harvest Lane NE Thompson ND 58278
or email at nancyyoshida@live.com

For permission on the artwork contact: Jon Van Zyle
PO Box 770746, Eagle River, Alaska 99577
or email at alaskaunitededitions@gmail.com

ISBN-061555764
Printing at Forum Communications Printing, Fargo ND
www.forumprinting.com

Books can be ordered at nigelschoice@hotmail.com

Nigel's Choice-My Iditarod Adventure
By Nancy Yoshida

Art work by Jon Van Zyle

Edited by Diane Johnson and Liza Kollman
Title by Diane Johnson

Table of Contents

Dedication

This book is dedicated to Mark Kelliher. A mentor in HAM Radio, a friend, and the strength behind Nigel's rescue. Mark's dedication to Iditarod over the years in the areas of Communications and Logistics have allowed the race to become what it is today. I know he is in a better place now, and I hope we will meet again on that final trail. 73's, my dear friend.

Nigel's Choice
My Iditarod Adventure

Flash Back

5,4,3,2,1 and they were off. Mike was running down the trail in his first race. We were in Frazee, Minnesota, only a few hours from our home in North Dakota. I was excited for him and felt confident that he would be safe with his lead dog Trumsa, who would guide him along the race route and across the finish line. Trumsa, was a special dog that Mike had bought from a famous musher, Susan Butcher. When she sold Trumsa to Mike to be his first lead dog, Susan told me she had been one of her best. Our life with sled dogs, and our eventual entrance in The Last Great Race began there.

Our Choices

Definition: choice: a decision made.

In 1996, we moved to North Dakota and began our kennel. The year before we made the move, our son Michael, who was five, saw the movie "Iron Will." When Mike saw an article from the Grand Forks Herald Newspaper in the movie, he thought of his father Glen, who would be working at the clinic in Grand Forks. Mike's first comment was "Mom, when we move to Grand Forks, can we get sled dogs too?" The rest is history; because at the moment those words were spoken we had made our choices that would lead us to the Last Great Race, Iditarod. I just didn't know it yet.

We felt we were fortunate to meet Vern Halter and Susan Whiton early in our mushing experience. They helped Mike get some great dogs and gave him direction about mushing. This developed into a lasting friendship. We had already become friends with Susan Butcher and David Monson as Mike decided on his first lead dog. We were fortunate to have advice from some world-renowned mushers at an early point in our mushing career.

When Michael began intramural sports in middle school, the dogs became my own passion. I began training and quickly decided I liked mid-distance better than sprint racing. All of the adventures I had and choices I made along the way led me to standing on the runners of the sled beneath the starting banner at the 2009 Iditarod. After all my hard work my goal was to get to Nome and finish the race. But this race became about Nigel's choice, not mine. Here is Nigel's story.

Preface by Nancy Yoshida

It no longer mattered what time it was, or how long I had been on the trail between Finger Lake and Rainy Pass. I moved on, looking back over my shoulder, hopeful to get a glimpse of Nigel. He was not to be seen. I decided to continue down the trail toward Rainy Pass. Each time my sled crashed I encouraged the team forward and comforted them for the hard work they'd accomplished. I was thankful for the way they'd stayed with me on the trail, yet I was hesitant to leave without Nigel. My heart was heavy from this journey. It had started so right and had so suddenly changed. At the same time, my heart was light. Although I was physically there on the trail and feeling the pain of being slammed into the ground over and over, I knew I was also with Nigel, wherever he was. I hoped he could feel me and my thoughts for him. I hoped he knew I just wanted him with us, safe and sound. He had made his choice because of the circumstances that led him there. I still had my choice to make, which was to get the rest of the team to Rainy Pass, and then to find Nigel.

Chapter 1

Moving to North Dakota by Nigel an Alaskan Sled Dog

It all began several years ago, when my brother and I were sold to Nancy. We were yearlings and had only raced one time before we went to live in North Dakota. I must say, North Dakota was a lot different from our first home in Wisconsin. There were no pine tree forests; there were only plains full of wheat, and Mother Nature's famous winds of the Dakotas. We soon learned all about working hard in harsh conditions, as well as working as a team. We soon learned that the wind sometimes made challenges and other times was our friend.

Our new Mom Nancy seemed nice, and we soon settled into the routine. There were probably 22 other dogs in the kennel. The food was different than what we'd been used to, but it was good none the less. My brother and I sure loved to eat. Our new Mom was just starting out in distance racing. She had participated in a few races and was learning more all the time. It seemed like a good place for my brother and me to settle down and develop our own sled dog skills.

Sorry, I forgot my manners! I should introduce myself to you. My name is Nigel and my brother is Mr. Ray. We were named from characters in "Finding Nemo." We are Alaskan Huskies and we just love to pull dogsleds. That is all we can think about doing, and when we get to run and pull we have the best time ever.

After several years of running races, pulling sleds, and sleeping in our dog houses in North Dakota, and after we competed in many races, our mom Nancy decided we were going to race the BIG ONE, the Iditarod. It takes a lot of time, effort, and money to do a race that long. I heard mom say once that it cost about $60,000 to compete in the Last Great Race. Mom had been to Alaska, read lots of books, and talked to many people about her goals. She'd been following the race for quite a few years so she knew a lot of information about the race. She didn't make the decision to run lightly. One thing about Mom is that when she makes up her mind, she makes up her mind, and her determination and energy about racing in Iditarod made me proud to call her Mom.

Once the decision was made to do it, Mom began to work out the logistics of racing Iditarod. She made arrangements to stay at her friend's kennel in Alaska. Her friends, Vern and Susan, would help get us all ready for the race. They had both run the Iditarod many times and knew all about getting a team ready. They also knew how to pack drop bags. There was plenty of room at Vern's for her to live, and lots of space in the dog yard for us. Mom knew that it would all work out pretty well. From the dog yard, we watched her making choices and decisions, talking to friends and family, and setting about making lots of plans.

Mom packed up the dog trailer in October and planned to leave for Alaska on the 21st. Packing the trailer was no easy task. My brother and I, along with the rest of the dogs at the kennel, watched with amazement as Mom and her friends worked so hard day after day, getting things ready for the very long drive from North Dakota. It would take us through Canada and on to Alaska. From the stories she told us, and from what we overheard in the dog yard, we could only imagine what a great adventure this long trip and the months of training before us would be. Sometimes, we howled silly songs in the dog yard while we watched our human family prepare for the journey. We couldn't believe all of the stuff she was taking with us. I wondered if there would be room for us, too. We didn't want to be left behind.

Oh the stuff that got packed! Mom had ordered about 3,000 booties and packed them for the trip. She also packed our jackets and blankets, 20 bags of dry kibble, 400 pounds of beaver meat, our gang line with all the tug lines and necklines attached, spare tug lines and necklines, plastic for the runners, drop lines, and the list went on and on. As you can imagine, it was not an easy task to get ready to leave for a race. We dogs were exhausted watching the work. Back and forth they'd wander, from the kennel to the dog barn, to the house, and back again. They were making lists, counting, organizing, sometimes laughing, and sometimes shaking their heads.

Mom also took two sleds. One was a basket sled and one was a trailer sled. Next, she had to load all of her personal mushing gear. This included boots, hats, gloves, neck gaiters, and many different weight coats. There was also a box of long-johns of different weights, not to mention her everyday wear. Mom's favorite color is purple, so you can guess what color we saw a lot of while the clothing and gear was being loaded into the trailer. We found it hard to believe that she'd need that much clothing along, but we kept hearing her talking about the race and how long it would be. We also heard about the vast wilderness we'd travel through, so the clothing made sense. Plus, we'd be living at Vern's kennel from the time we got to Alaska until we came back to North Dakota after the race.

Sometimes, while we watched them organize and pack, I daydreamed. I dreamed about the Alaskan trails we'd run on, the animals we'd see, the mountains we'd climb, the weather we'd face, and how everything would be different. Mom was busy reading books, talking to people, learning everything she could, and making phone calls to finalize details. All I could do was use my imagination.

The whole packing process seemed to take a lot longer than we dogs wanted it to take. Luckily, Mom's friends Sue and Boyd were there to help. Otherwise I don't think she would have gotten it all done. Sue and Boyd are friends that help Mom in the dog yard, along with Cameron.

Oh, and there were things we had to help with too. Some of them weren't so fun! We had to go to the vet and get checked over from the tips of our noses to the tips of our tails. Some of us even had to have shots, and those of us who would come due for Rabies had to have boosters too. When we went to the Vet's office, Cameron came along with Mom to help load and unload us. You would think we were unruly or something, with all the help Mom thinks she needs sometimes! I personally don't like to get shots, but I'm brave, and truthfully, they don't hurt a bit. But don't tell Mom!

At long last, it seemed that Mom checked off the last item on her list, and it was finally time for the journey to Alaska to begin. We could hardly sleep the night before we left and so we ran extra circles around our dog houses. Maybe we understood about the long ride and long naps we'd have on the trip. Maybe we understood we would really start working hard again once we got to Alaska, so we'd better enjoy the R and R! Maybe we had all imagined so many things, watched so much packing, and listened to so many stories that we were just too excited to sleep.

Mom's best friend Leora came from Washington D.C. to drive with us up to Alaska. On the day we left we went to the vet to get our final distemper shots and to pick up our health certificates. Those papers were pretty important because we needed them to cross the border into Canada on our way to Alaska. I was amazed with Mom because she remembered so many details! Like I said, I was proud of her!

When everything seemed to be done, finally, we dogs howled a sigh of relief in a very long dog song howl because it was at last time to head to Alaska. It is a very long drive, and in fact, it took us seven days of driving about 12 hours each day. While we traveled we heard Mom and Leora talk about the beautiful drive. From what we could see of it, it was beautiful. But, it was very slow going. Mom took such good care of us on the drive. She made sure to stop every three hours. Our travel boxes were cozy and comfy, but after three hours we were all ready to get out and stretch, as well as do our business!

In the Yukon Territory there were long stretches of road with frost boils that made it very slow going. Mom and Leora saw many animals on the trip, including wild buffalo, caribou, eagles, owls, moose, and elk. The long stretches between potty breaks gave us plenty of time to dream about the adventures before us. Mom and Leora had plenty of time to visit and catch up. Those two certainly like to chat! They'd go on and on about such interesting things, like their homes, dreams, plans and ideas, and also the scenery! Mom was always talking about learning things, too. One thing she learned on the trip was never to pass a gas station while in Alberta or the Yukon Territory without putting some fuel in the tank. She even bought a gas can while she was there and kept it full for the rest of the trip to Vern's. She only had to use it once, but she was very glad she had it.

After seven days of driving, we finally arrived at Vern's. Vern's handlers, Dee Dee and Misha helped Mom and Leora get us all out of our dog boxes. They put each of us on a chain at a new dog house. We ran around the houses after our long ride and sniffed and sniffed, and did our business. We were so excited because everything was new to us. There was a new dog yard, with new dogs already there, and new human voices all around us. Even the sky looked different. It was all very confusing and Mom wasn't very comfortable with all of us moving without her help. She's a good Mom, but sometimes I think she is a little too overprotective. I'm sure you all know what I'm talking about because maybe your Mom is the same way. She's always keeping an eye on you to keep you safe. That's what Moms do. They don't feel good when you are out of their sight for too long, they don't want you to get lost. As soon as my paws touched the ground at Vern's house, I made up my mind: I was there to have a great adventure!

Chapter 2

Training Choices
and Adventures

At Vern's kennel, our new home, we each had a house and a circle. That means that each of use had our own doghouse, and we were tethered to a pole next to the house. Our chain made it possible for each of us to get lots and lots of exercise by running around and around our circles.

Once we were settled at our new houses, we were greeted with a great meal. I must say that the food at Vern's was much better than I could ever imagine. We only had kibble while on the long journey, and it got to be the "same old, same old" if you know what I mean. I'm not saying it was bad. I'm a fella that loves my kibble, but it did get boring. Our new dinner here at Vern's consisted of beef, liver, and kibble, and it was great. A few bites into the meal I really wanted to start the whole dog yard howling in a delightful yummy song. But, I didn't want to make my new friends who'd already been living at Vern's dog yard think I was bossy or a know-it-all. I couldn't help but to bark to my traveling fur buddies "I think I am going to like it here if we keep eating this way!" Back home in North Dakota, Mom had always fed us a lot of beaver and deer, but we only got beef when we were racing. I decided if the food was always going to be this good I was really going to like living in Alaska. Right away I started to dream about my next meal.

Vern was Mom's friend and mushing mentor. He was also the boss of Dream a Dream Dog Farm. This was the place where we were going to live. He had been at a meeting when we arrived, so after we ate we ran around our circles, sniffing and enjoying our new home. When Vern got home, we all got to go for a run at the front of a snow machine! We had never done that before and it was a new experience for all of us, my mom included.

We couldn't believe what was about to happen! We were nervous, excited, and raring to go. Mom was suddenly driving a snow machine with a dog team and we could tell she was not as confident in driving a snow machine as she was in driving a dog sled. We could see she was a little shaken with this new experience. The trails we would be running were new to Mom, and everything seemed to be happening so fast. Mom was also nervous because of the hills and dips on the trail that we didn't have at home in North Dakota. Have I told you about how flat it is back home? It is! But in Alaska, it was so different. There was very little flat there at all. We were so proud of Mom because she survived this first adventure, but it was really scary for all of us. This experience made us remember something that Mom had said to us before we left home – that we'd all be learning a lot of new things, even Mom. I guess the snow machine was just one of those new things.

The best part of getting back to our new home after the scary run was getting a really nice yummy treat. This was another type of food we didn't get at home. At home we got beaver or deer meat when we were done working. The snack at Vern's was a combination of kibble, meat, frozen together with water. It was sort of like a soup only frozen. I quickly seconded my earlier prediction that things were going to be just fine around here, since the taste of things around the kennel were pretty delicious. You know we dogs decide most things by our stomach. If the food is good and plentiful, and the talk is nice, we are very happy. A good meal can always make the scary go away. The dreams of a fun run and lots of yummy meals fill in the scary spaces!

The next day, the morning routine started with everyone helping in the kennel. Misha, Vern's handler, would get our breakfast ready in the mornings. I heard Mom say she came from the Czech Republic. I don't know where that is, I just know it is a long way from Alaska. Dee Dee was the one who took care of Vern's older dogs, or dogs who were in the clinic. Vern's wife, Susan, was the vet, and she took care of dog patients who were on rest in her clinic.

For us, the morning routine started with more of that good food. It was so delicious that it made me howl with happiness. Then Mom, Leora, Misha, and Dee Dee started "picking the dog yard." If you don't know what that is, just imagine what 60 well-fed sled dogs can produce in their circles overnight. That's what the picking job is all about. It is very important because sometimes we dogs get into the bad habit of eating our poop if it isn't removed from our yard and circle. I know, it sounds kind of icky, but it's a dog thing. Humans don't like us to do it, so they get to picking and picking until the dog yard is cleaned up spic and span.

We were all relaxing after the meal and the picking was complete when suddenly we noticed there was a strange dog truck in the yard. We were all getting into it to go for a ride. I didn't know whose truck it was, but we were all going somewhere even through we'd just finished a long ride from North Dakota to Alaska. We were heading out again! Since our Mom wasn't helping to load us, we were a little scared and not sure we wanted to go. After all, Alaska was a new world to us, and the people that we were just getting to know seemed to be in charge. Where was Mom? Was she going too? We were hesitant, but more than a little curious.

To our relief, Mom showed up finally, and everything felt

OK again. The unsettled feeling in my stomach was gone because I always know that when I'm with Mom, things are just fine. Don't get me wrong, I'm not a momma's boy. I'm confident and brave on my own, but there's nobody like Mom. She's the one who feeds us. But more than that, she loves us no matter what! I trust her with my life and I'd do anything for her.

We traveled in the truck to a different trail than the first one we'd worked on yesterday. We had lots of help to get our harnesses on and to get lined out in front of Vern's big four wheel cart. This was new, too. Not the cart so much, but having so many helpers. Mostly, Mom had done this on her own before or with the help of Boyd and Sue. Cameron also used to help get us ready to work. This helped us understand that there were lots of humans that cared for us and they were going to help us learn all that we needed to learn before we could take Mom on that run from Anchorage to Nome that they all kept talking about.

This wheeled cart was very different from the four-wheeler we used at home. Mom, Vern, and Leora could all ride in it at once. Misha and Dee Dee stayed with the truck, but I think they could probably have ridden in it too, but I'm sort of glad they didn't. Having three humans on the cart was plenty heavy for this run. We ran for about eight miles and then returned to the truck. We got some more of those yummy kibble snacks with beef and liver. I knew I was going to like it here! I wagged my tail and did a little dance to show how much I loved those snacks! Then, they unharnessed us and put us back in the truck. We all headed back to the kennel. I overheard Vern tell Mom that he thought we all looked good and were pulling just like we should. I had wanted to make Mom proud, and I knew she was. Since Mom had never worked in a professional kennel before, we could tell there were going to be tough training days before us. But, that second day had been a good start!

After we returned to the kennel, we all took a nap until dinner. Yes, we did get that good beef and kibble meal again. I realized that it might be the main course at the kennel and I really howled to everyone about how I liked the menu this place had to serve to us. I couldn't help but hope that after this long adventure was over and we got back home again Mom would continue to feed it to us.

I wondered about the beef that Vern fed us, and if Mom could get that beef back home. I wondered where all of the snacks came from, after spying a huge freezer full of frozen treats. I wondered what my favorite snack would be. I wondered about the other dogs in the dog yard, and I took long sniffs in the air. I could smell good human food being cooked up in the bunk house where Mom was staying. I wondered about all sorts of things, and soon I was fast asleep and dreaming. I had a scary dream, one of me being out on the trail, all alone, with no Mom, no rest of the team, and even worse, no yummy treats. I woke with a startle, so happy to be safe in my dog house in my own circle and not all alone on the trail. I promised myself that I would stick with Mom and not wander off no matter what.

Chapter 3

Training can be Hard

The next morning after the howling, the eating, and the daily chores, Vern and Mom took out a twenty dog team with a snow machine. I watched as the dogs were chosen, but none of Mom's dogs got harnessed. I was puzzled and curious, but then I was glad that it was Vern's dogs on the gang line because Mom seemed a little nervous. It looked like it was time for Mom to have some training without us, so we all howled a song to cheer her on as they left the yard. The moment they left, I wondered more about how that run would go and tried to imagine myself on the gang line too. I then took a dog yard snooze.

When they finally got back I could tell from the attitude that the humans had, and the way the dogs grumbled as they went back to their houses, something wasn't quite right. I soon heard it was not the best run ever. Vern had let my mom drive and she had a really hard time with all of the hills and the uneven ground covered with snow and ice. I heard her saying that she made a mistake coming up one of the hills, and rolled the snow machine over, throwing Vern down the hill. I can only imagine what this would have looked like, how it would have sounded, and how it would have felt to be involved in the whole training adventure. I wondered and wondered, and then tried not to think about it. She probably wouldn't be happy that I told you, but I hoped that we never had to do that with her.

After hearing her story, the humans disappeared and went in to have lunch. We all relaxed. Even the dogs back from the adventure were ready for a snooze, almost like they'd forgotten what had happened. But not me. Just as all thoughts of what had happened out there were replaced by good thoughts about winning a race, suddenly the humans were back in the dog yard. Things were about to get busy again and I thought about taking shelter in my dog house for awhile.

"Oh dear! They are coming to put our harnesses on and now they are hooking us to that machine!" I could hardly stand to think about it. We thirteen from our kennel and three from Vern's were hooked up and ready to go. Yes, Mom was driving and Aunt Leora was on the back. "Here we go down another new trail!"

On the first steep, rutted hill that we came to, Mom turned the snow machine half over. But, we were able to continue. No one was hurt, just unsettled by the near tip. I wondered how long it would take her before she learned to drive the snow machine. Would she learn at all?

I know that at some point, I heard Vern say "It's going to be a long winter!"The rest of our work on that run was uneventful, but it was scary none the less. I wondered and I worried what Mom was going to do next. We sled dogs like to know that our drivers know what's going on, and in this situation I wasn't sure our mom did. I kept wondering and wondering as we ran, and was very happy to arrive back at my dog house for a good long snooze.

Chapter 4

Patience, Practice, and Persistence

Halloween is supposed to be scary. For us, it was another exciting day around our new kennel.

Mom got up early and took Aunt Leora to the airport. After she got back to the kennel and finished morning chores, she, Misha and Dee Dee started to harness a sixteen-dog team to run the twenty-miles we had done the previous day, again. We were going to run in front of the snow machine. Some of you might call this a snowmobile. Mom was driving and Misha was the passenger. I was full of wonder but of course, like all the dogs on the team, I showed my eagerness to run. No matter what had happened before, this was an adventure and was going to be fun!

It started out fine. We left the yard and the dogs who weren't going sang a howl song for us as we left, cheering us on. I was so happy that there were no problems getting out of the yard and I had good thoughts that this run would be better than the one the day before had been. I like exciting runs, but I'd rather not have any problems! About two miles out, the dogs in lead position were doing a good job, but the dogs in swing position, Oslo, and her partner, East, were having problems. Mom had to stop twice because of disagreements they were having, and it made me a little nervous because I wasn't sure what to expect. After that she made the decision to separate them and all was going very well. I could tell that Misha was nervous on the hills and was making Mom drive a certain way. Of course, there was a conflict with what Vern said to Mom about driving, and what Misha thought about driving on the hills, so there were some tense moments.

Once we got into the swamp, we slowed way down because of too much ice. All seemed to be going well until we were a few miles away from the turnaround. We went down a small icy dip and the snow machine tossed both Mom and Misha off. Now, I'm not sure what really happened but suddenly I realized that we were continuing on our own, just the snow machine and us. There was no Misha and there was no Mom. Mom didn't have the kill switch attached to her so the machine didn't shut off. We were all in a thought provoking position. We dogs on the team didn't seem to be near as stressed as Mom and Misha were.

Mom called the kennel and left a message about the situation. Susan, Vern's wife, called back, but not until after everything had been resolved so Mom and Misha didn't get any help. Misha cut across the trail to see if she could get back to the return trail and Mom continued to follow us. After 30 minutes, give or take a few, of walking and running to catch up to us, Misha got to the other trail and was able to stop us. She pulled all our tugs and just waited for Mom to arrive. Thank God no one was hurt, except for Mom's pride. I could not believe this happened. "It may not be my mom's best suit to drive snow machines," I thought, and I wondered how much longer we would have runs like this before we got to pull a sled.

After Mom caught up and she and Misha had some time to calm down, we continued on our way. Misha continued to be uneasy with Mom's driving. Mom was trying to do what Vern said, but Misha was really upset as we were going down a very steep treacherous spot in the trail. She was tapping Mom on her back and telling her to break. When she finally did break it flipped the snow machine in a hole and yes, Mom lost us again. This time the snow machine did not fare too well. I couldn't believe the sight. The snow machine had no mirrors and a broken windshield. I could tell there was a little tension in the Alaskan air.

Needless to say, Mom felt very incompetent – and we felt a little sad. Misha called the kennel and Vern came to pick us up. Misha was wary and unsure of Vern's driving too, so it made for an uncomfortable ride. Vern had stopped us and hooked us down, undoing our tugs before he went to find Mom and Misha. Vern is an excellent snow machine driver and dog trainer. Mom didn't have any problem with what he was doing. After they caught up to us, they connected the tugs and Vern drove us the rest of the way home.

After we all got home, Mom snacked us. Then she put us back at our houses. Mom, Misha and Dee Dee lined out the second team. This time, Vern took them, but told Mom and Misha where to meet him so they could cut a new trail to avoid the steep and dangerous spot on the trail that had caused Mom so much trouble. I was happy to see them leave. It sounded like they'd be making a better trail that we could train on. We thought they'd be gone a long time, so we had plenty of time to snooze and wonder about what we were doing. I was sure glad about the delicious snacks and meals that we were being served while we were in Alaska. Other than that, I would have started to wonder what we were doing in this new place.

Misha drove the snow machine as she took off with Mom, and we watched. They were on the way to meet Vern where he'd said to. They didn't have to wait very long at the appointed meeting spot before he came. He took the snow machine that they were on, and told Mom to drive the team. On his snow machine there was a box that houses a gas powered saw to cut any obstacles out of his way. Mom did fine when she drove the machine. They made it back without having any other problems. Mom told us about her day while she fed us, and then she went into the bunk house to relax.

I found out later that when Mom went back inside, there was a Halloween treat waiting for her from her husband Glen. He'd sent her a big box of pears, apples, and cheese. I knew that Mom's spirit would be lifted from this gift, and she really needed it after what she'd been through.

I knew that getting Mom to where she needed to be with all the new experiences was going to test Vern's patience and teaching skills. But Mom is not a quitter. I could already tell that Vern wasn't a quitter either. I thought that mom and Vern were a lot alike. I knew that Mom would keep working at it until she figured it all out. I liked to listen to the humans when they were all talking together, so I can know what's going on. Mom told Vern that she thought she was a better dog sled driver than snow machine driver. I dreamed of snow that night as I went to sleep, so that we could pull the sled and not the snow machine.

Chapter 5

Showing Resilience

We continued to train four times a week. The distances increased every third time, until we were running fifty miles at a time. We planned on entering the race at Sheep Mountain Lodge in early December. Mom and Vern were both going to drive a team so it would be a lot of work. But, it would be a lot of fun, too. We love to race, and racing with another team from the same dog yard would make it a lot of fun. Vern told Mom that it would be a chance for her to get some great experience, because that trail is steep and interesting. It had lots of hills, plenty that were steep and challenging. It sounded fun but I had never been on really steep hills going downhill, so I was worrying and wondering as we trained for the race. When we were racing in Montana, we never had to worry about any awful downhill trails, so I decided it was going to be fun. When Mom wasn't listening I told my fur friends "I bet we can scare Mom if we try really hard." They all agreed, and we all howled about it for quite some time!

In Vern's yard, there were several dogs that could run in lead. Some were from our kennel, and some were from Vern's kennel. Mom sometimes had trouble with the leaders from Vern's kennel because they were used to his style of driving and not hers. Every musher has his own style of driving. Vern was more direct with his commands, saying to turn right, "gee", or turn left, "haw" right at the turn, not before. She didn't have any trouble with dogs from our kennel, because we were used to her style. I knew that Vern's dogs would get used to Mom's way of doing things soon, but those first few rides were exciting with this miscommunication. Maybe exciting is the wrong word to use. I think it was more frustrating for Mom, and funny for us.

We weren't at the kennel for very long when it started to get cold enough to see hoar frost. If you don't know what it is, it's a frost that causes the trees to turn white and frosty. It makes the world beautiful and lets you know that snow must be coming.

I asked mom what causes the frost. She said it was because the ground is warmer than the air, and that causes the warm air to rise in the form of water vapor. It sticks on the trees forming pretty crystals as it goes by. It sounded really complicated, but that's what Mom told me.

We loved the snow falling, because we knew it meant that mom and Vern could get a trail packed down so we could run with the dogsleds. You need to have a nice hard packed trail when you run dogsleds. Mom has a good snow hook to keep us stopped. It looks like an anchor and it keeps us stopped when she needs to give us a snack, or even when she just needs to stop and say hi to us. She does that a lot, and it keeps us happy. If there isn't enough snow to use the snow hook, we might just run off with or without Mom. She wouldn't be very happy if we did that, so she always makes sure that the trail is hard packed before we go out on a sled.

When there's more snow, it means the trails are better and the dogs AND the humans are happy!

Chapter 6

Dog Baths, Training and Moose

Not too many days later, Vern arrived in the dog barn in the morning. He told Mom, Dee Dee, and Misha that we were going to wash the dogs. Some of us like baths, and some of us don't. So, bath time is always interesting in the dog yard!

Misha got out two tubs, and filled them both with warm water. The parade of dogs began. Mom and Vern did the washing. Misha and Dee Dee gathered all of us dogs together. I must say, it was a wild event. They brought us in the door and put us in a big tub. Then, they put soap on us, and scrubbed us. After that, they put us into another tub that had warm water to rinse the soap off of us. After that, they took us outside so we could frolic and go back to our houses. Bath time was a fun time for us! I'm not sure the people had as much fun as we did. They had soggy clothes on, but we were having a blast. Once outside, we shook and rolled to get the water off before they put us back on our chains. The entire day was filled with fun and games, as far as I was concerned!

The weather must have known that we were all clean, because the next day it got really cold, and we didn't feel the same kind of warm again until Spring. The ground became harder and harder, the wind became colder and colder, and it was clear. The season of real training and racing had arrived!

Once the snow really began, Mom was busy working with Vern every day. They worked on the trails all the time, packing them down so we could really use sleds. Mom wouldn't take us out on a sled, until there was a lot of hard packed snow. She never found it funny when we ran away if the snow wasn't deep enough for a snow hook to hold the team. We always looked back and grinned, but she never grinned back!

November 17 was just another day for us. I'm not really sure what that calendar date means, but I do know we went out on the trails with sleds. Going out on the trails is always fun. On this day, though, it brought back a few memories. We were not out very long when we saw three moose very close to the trail. I know that Mom was concerned as I heard her give us commands. But, everything was fine. I have heard her tell the story of a moose coming through her team when she was racing the Beargrease 150 a few years back. I guess she was pretty shook up and scared by the experience. After that, she hated to see Moose on the trail. We always pay close attention when we know Mom is concerned so she doesn't have to worry so much. We might joke and laugh when we dump her off the sled and leave her behind, but moose are never something to joke about. Moose are not a friend to sled dogs, but a danger.

As the days went by, the training continued on sleds, and it just got better and better. The snow kept coming down and the trails were wonderful. We all worked pretty well together. It was like one big happy family with Vern's dogs and Mom's dogs. We all trained together, worked together, and played together. Plus, we all had hearty appetites, and snoozed together in our dog houses. We spent our time wondering about wonderful things, like races along the Iditarod Trail with the Northern Lights above us. We were born to run and trained to run. It is our life, and we love every minute of it!

During the first weekend in December, Mom headed to Anchorage for the rookie meeting. All rookies have to attend this meeting if they plan on entering the next race. The rookie meeting includes a meeting with the Iditarod Head

Veterinarian, the Communications Director, the Public Relations Director, and others. Finally Musher Martin Buser, a four time winner, gives a presentation. Mom enjoyed the meeting very much, and was impressed by Martin Buser's generosity in sharing all of the information he did with everyone. She also had a chance to meet all the other rookies she'd be racing with. Mom shared all of the details with us, and they made us just as pleased as she was. After all, we were planning a great adventure that would start soon, and everything we had been doing and would do from then on was all about getting ready to race. Sometimes, I almost forgot all about North Dakota because I was too busy wondering about what it would be like to race to Nome.

Mom was pleased when she got back after the rookie meetings, and we started training again right away the next Monday. Vern started to go through Mom's gear, and told her to order some new items before we did the Sheep Mountain race. Vern was taking a team for that race too, for training, so he was planning for it too. He thought it would be a good time for Mom to test her sled driving abilities. After we did the race, I agreed. It was really challenging, with very steep up and downs. Mom was pleased with the way we performed, and she was feeling more confident about everything as each day went by.

Chapter 7

Winter and the Christmas Holiday

Mom went back to North Dakota for Christmas, but before she left she and Vern planned a Christmas party for everyone at the kennel, and all of Vern's neighbors too. Mom and Vern made a ham, sweet potatoes, mashed potatoes, green bean casserole, and homemade sugar cookies. There was also peppermint ice cream. Misha and Dee Dee cut down a Christmas tree and decorated it in the dog barn. I don't know why we didn't get any treats, but I know that everyone who came had a good time. The next day, Mom went home to North Dakota for Christmas. I knew we would miss her while she was gone, and we were sad to see her leave. But, we knew that she would have a good Christmas seeing Glen, Mike, and all of the friends we'd left behind. I wished we could all go, but knew it would take too long to drive us home and back again, so we stayed. While she was gone, we did some training runs, but mostly rested. We knew that when she got back, it would be time to get our noses to the grindstone.

Mom came back on January 2nd. It had snowed a lot while she was gone, and it was very cold. It stayed that way for awhile, but then it got really warm, and a lot of the snow melted. It was crazy! Sheep Mountain was the only place that had snow, so Mom, Vern, and Misha took us there to do some training runs. We enjoyed seeing those beautiful trails again and liked being where it was cold and snowy.

Vern said that this was something that happened every year in January. All the snow goes away, but then it comes back again. It was sure hard to train when all the snow was gone. It was hard to feed us, and pick up the dog yard, because the ground was solid ice. Mom liked it though, because we could work over lakes covered by overflow, which was the kind of work we couldn't do at home. We hadn't seen overflow before, so it was good to have the experience. Mom was smart and wanted us to know as much as we could know about the trail conditions in Alaska. When we did it for the first time, Mom was pleased that we handled it so well. Kirin and the other leaders did not seem stressed by it, so the rest of us weren't either. We just followed as we should, and faced the challenges. Mom had confidence in herself and in all of us, so everything we did while training was making us into the best Iditarod team we could be.

We stayed out at Sheep Mountain for two nights, and got a lot of running in, so our confidence and our skills continued to grow. Mom and Misha camped out on the trail for one night, and it was so much fun. Mom cooked for us, and even had straw there that we could rest on. Mom hadn't taken the straw on the sled, so we guessed that Vern had brought it on the snow machine. We were supposed to go on another run in the morning, but when Mom got up she didn't feel well, so we went home to work another day.

There were many things that we had to do before the start of the race. Food drops is an important part of the Iditarod, and Mom had to take care of that before we could go. Mom had ordered many things for the race. She ordered a new Anorak and pants, but they hadn't come yet.

She was concerned because the one she had was old, and it wasn't that warm any more. The one thing no one wants is to be cold on the trail. Mom had also bought many pairs of wool socks. "The more wool the better!" she said many times. She was shopping at all of the second hand stores for as many wool sweaters she could buy so she could pack them in her sled and send them out on the trail. She told us that not only did she have to pack the sled for the race, but she also had to plan what was needed for the checkpoints.

Mom had to pack everything she needed out on the trail into bags and label them, and then drive them to Anchorage so they could be flown out on the trail. It is no easy task to pack those bags. Vern had raced Iditarod many times, and his wife Susan had raced too, so they knew everything there was to know about this big important job. All of the meat for meals and snacks had to be cut and put in bags. Our kibble had to be packed so that healthy and complete meals would be waiting on the trail for us when we arrived. Mom had to pack dry clothes, batteries for her headlamp, and food for herself, as well as booties, foot salve, and oil too. It took several days to do it right, and Vern drove Mom crazy because he kept dumping the bags and making her repack them. It was irritating, but he wanted to make sure Mom knew what was in each one. It made us smile to see them going around about all kinds of things, but we knew that Vern only wanted Mom to know exactly what she was doing.

After the bags were packed, Mom drove them to Anchorage. Then, they were sorted and weighed, so they could be shipped out to the various check points. We were glad to see the bags getting out to where they were supposed to be, but we knew that meant that we needed to be training and learning everything we could, because the race was getting closer. Race time was before us, and we wanted to know everything we were supposed to know. We had questions, too, so sometimes we made little mistakes on our runs, which was our way of asking questions. Then, the humans would talk about what we'd done, and we could practice telling them what we needed by what we did on our training runs.

We were working four times a week to get ready for the race. We usually did a 50 mile run and had a snack in the middle. We were getting pretty excited about the race and couldn't believe how fast the time was moving.

In the middle of February, Vern hosted a junior race at the kennel. It was a lot of fun. It was a 100 mile race that started and ended at Vern's. Mom made a gingerbread checkpoint house and put it on a table for the kids. It looked really cute, and the kids were talking about it. It was fun to watch a race even if we weren't in it, but soon we were thinking that it was time to get racing ourselves. All of the commotion was a lot of fun and all of the kids had a great time. Vern made biscuits and gravy for the kids in the morning, and Mom made chili for the end of the race. The parents had also made food, so everyone ate pretty well.

A boy named Travis won the race. He did a very good job and seemed very happy with his accomplishments. I hoped that we didn't have to watch too many more races though, because it was more fun when WE got to race. I could tell that Mom was getting excited for the race. The big day was quickly approaching. We all knew it. We dreamed about it. We were almost ready for it!

Finally, Mom's new Anorak and pants arrived. She was really pleased with them. She must have been warm because she looked really fat when she had them on. Don't tell her I said she looked fat, though! I thought those pants were going to be much better for her than her old ones.

Mom doesn't like bibs, because it's too hard to remove them when nature calls. We don't have that problem, we can just go whenever we want when we are running, but it isn't the same for her. The new pants zipped completely off, which is good for her. The anorak came down to her knees, so it kept out the wind. A few days after she got it, she had to drive to Anchorage to have her fur ruff sewn on. That looked really great too. I must say myself, although I've always known that Mom was a real musher, but, when I saw her all dressed up she really looked the part. Seeing her all dressed up like an Iditarod musher made us more excited about the race!

Chapter 8

February and the Race

On February 19th, Mom and Misha took us to the Iditarod Headquarters so we could get our EKG's done and so we could get physicals and microchips. Susan came with us, and that made the process go very quickly. It was amazing to be put on a table and have all kinds of wires attached to us. Mom kept us calm, and it didn't really hurt. It made us more curious because we'd never had this kind of exam back in North Dakota. Mom had some paperwork, and got all of the micro chip numbers for identification. Then, we were done. After that, we got back in the trailer and headed home to the kennel.

The race was going to start on March 7th in Anchorage. Mom had to be there on March 4th so she could meet her Idita-Rider and be at the musher meeting. Glen, Mom's husband, and Mike, her son, came down the night before. They all went to the banquet, where the starting order would be drawn. Some of Mom's friends flew to Alaska to be there for the banquet too, and also the start of the race. Things were getting more and more busy, and more and more serious. We knew that soon we'd be racing to Nome.

The humans were busy with people things, and we dogs were busy remembering all of the things we'd practiced so we'd be ready for the race to start. Mom told us about everything she was doing, so we could stay in the know. We felt all the emotions she was feeling too, but we were also confident in her driving and mushing skills.

The Musher Meeting was exciting for Mom. At the musher meeting, she got her Trail Mail to sign. She signed it and gave it back, so it could be wrapped up and given back on race day so she'd have it with her in her sled bag from Anchorage to Nome. All the mushers got mail to carry to Nome. Each year, the design of the mail is different, and celebrates that particular Iditarod. Mom was excited to see it, but was disappointed because it was only an envelope face, not a real envelope. In the past, she had gotten some from other mushers and each was a piece of art. She also got letters from school children that she could answer, that had questions about why she liked to mush and how long it would take her to get to Nome. Mom likes to teach children about the Iditarod, and she likes to help them learn that they can and should reach for the sky for whatever their dreams are. She was very happy to answer questions from students.

After Mom signed all of the required items, it was time to hear from the race officials. They talked about the rule changes and the trail conditions, as well as the concerns of the Vet team, and important information about the race. It was exciting to be a part of it all in preparation for the big day. Mom spent lunch with her Idita-Rider Karen. Karen is a teacher and was excited to ride in the sled out of Anchorage. Mom assured her that it would be a great time and not to worry. Mike was going to be Mom's handler on the ride out of Anchorage. He had come from college in Connecticut, so he could be a part of it all. He had been the one to get this all started a long time before I was part of the family. Mom was proud of Mike and glad he was coming. She'd been worried that he might not make it there in time, but we knew he'd never miss out on it.

The lectures and meetings continued after lunch on Thursday, and finally ended in time for everyone to have a break before the banquet, which is where the starting positions are drawn. All of Mom's friends and family sat together at the banquet.

After the meeting ended, Mom and her husband Glen, as well as Mike and a lot of her friends like Leora headed to downtown Anchorage to go to the banquet. They wanted to be on time, and had to wait for the doors to open. Everyone visited in the lobby because there was a delay. After they got in, they had a great table that was close to the stage where the mushers would draw their start position. It also allowed them to watch the entertainment.

Hobo Jim sang his songs, and Lee Larson, the president of the Board of Directors, gave a nice welcome. Jim Lanier, his wife, and their son sang the national anthem. Jim is also an Iditarod musher who went to medical school in North Dakota when he was younger. Mom became friends with him the winter before we went to Alaska, and it was nice for her to hear him sing. His wife Anna had raced the Iditarod before. Their son Jimmy will probably do it someday too. Mom said the meal was great. Everyone wanted the meal to move along, so the bib draw could begin. Mom's son drew for her, and got the #3 spot. Mom wasn't sure she wanted to start in that position but there was no turning back. I wasn't concerned and thought it sounded great. We were excited that we wouldn't have to wait very long to run. The earlier the better if you ask me – the start of the race is always a hard time to wait.

The evening's official business was over at 9pm. During the rest of the time, spectators could visit and get autographs. Everyone who came to support Mom had a great time, and Mom did too. Mom, Glen, and Mike all stayed in town that night. They enjoyed not having to drive back to the kennel that evening, and enjoyed relaxing before the Ceremonial Start on Saturday. Glen and Mike came to the kennel on Friday and enjoyed the activities that Vern had planned. He had dogsled rides for anyone who wanted to go on one. We had a great time giving rides. Everyone was nice and showed us a lot of love. It was fun to have that kind of company. In a way, it felt like we were movie stars or something!

If you ask me, I could have had company like that every day! Those kind of days weren't stressful for us, just fun. We got treats when we came in, like always. Everyone who took a ride had a wonderful time. When everyone left, we all got into the dog trailer and headed towards Anchorage. We were going to stay at the same place Mom was staying so we would be ready early in the morning. After we arrived, we had dinner and then just rested. It looked like Anchorage was having a big fair. We could see lots of people and ice sculptures everywhere, and there was lots of excitement all around us.

We knew this was the real thing now. After our dinner, all the humans went to a dinner of their own at a Mexican restaurant. When they came back, they wished us a good night and we all got out of our boxes to do our business before everyone went to bed. We all wondered and dreamed about what was going to happen the next day.

Chapter 9

The Start

Saturday started early. We got our breakfast and then got back into the dog trailer. Around 7:30am, we headed towards 4th Street, where the Start would take place. Misha and Dee Dee drove us, and Vern and Susan followed in the car. Mom and Glen were supposed to come later, but Mom couldn't stand waiting so she showed up right away. We were glad when she got there because we knew it meant we were going somewhere fun. There were so many people stopping by the trailer and visiting with Mom. It was fun because Mike was there too. We saw interesting sights and people and smelled lots of delicious smells. Something that the humans called reindeer sausage smelled very good. We heard dogs barking, people laughing, and music coming from a loud speaker. I had fun people watching. This is a fun game my fur friends and I like to play. It was fun to see all of the people walking in the slushy snow. Some of the people were dressed like they were going out for the evening, and some were dressed in all types of animal skins. Some were even dressed like us. It was a lot of fun but soon became more serious.

A lady from Iditarod stopped by and asked Mom how many handlers she wanted. After Mom told her, someone took a scan machine to see if we really belonged there. I was not sure about those things that they had stuck in us at the vet check, but they can be read anytime someone has one of those scan machines. Mom told them the wrong dog once, and the tag didn't match what she'd said. Sometimes Mom can't tell us apart when she's stressed out and only looking at us through the trailer door. Soon though, she found the dog she wanted and all was good again. Whew!

Misha and Dee Dee were busy helping us get harnessed and ready to go. Mom didn't bootie us because it was a warm day. If it is too warm the snow sticks to the booties and it makes it hard to move. We can also hurt a wrist if the snow really builds up. We were leaving in 3rd position so we didn't have to wait very long. Karen, Mom's Idita-Rider, showed up and Mom gave her an extra jacket so she would stay warm. Mike got on the runners behind Mom and Karen was in the seat in the front of Vern's tourist sled. We were happy because we had all of the help we needed to get to the start safely.

Once at the starting line, time went so fast! Mom walked to the front and then walked to the back of the team and spoke to each of us as she did. She spoke to the handlers too. During this time, a voice on the loud speaker was talking about Mom. I tried to listen, but I knew that whatever the voice was saying wasn't important to me, so I tried to block out the distractions. After all, I was in the LAST GREAT RACE and although I'm not a lead dog, I'm the member of an awesome team. 5-4-3-2-1 and we were off!

Oh my goodness was it exciting! We were going down the street in downtown Anchorage. I suddenly realized that there were people everywhere. Mom seemed happy and waved to the crowd. Our first turn was off 4th Street and then onto Cordova. It was a 90 degree right turn, which was no problem because we had a pretty good snow base. We went down Cordova and down the big hill, and then we were in some woods. Then we had to cross a big road on a bridge with a chain link fence on the sides. It must have been for people because I didn't think a car would fit up there. Coyote and Cy were doing a good job listening to Mom so far. Then, we got into some more woods, and there were people all along the trail passing out water, cookies, and hotdogs for the humans. I couldn't help but think, "Hey! What about treats for us! We're the real athletes!" Mike was having a great time also. He helped us when we went up hills. I know he was having a good time. I heard him tell mom "I forgot how much fun this was!" I know it made Mom happy that Mike was enjoying riding out of Anchorage with her. I'd heard the story about "Iron Will" and how that made Mike want sled dogs. I'm sure neither of them dreamed then that this day would be as it was, a mother and a son, together, helping each other, with their dogs, starting the Last Great Race.

It didn't seem too long, and then we were at the Campbell airstrip, where we would drop our rider and then head back to the truck for a snack. We would ride back to the kennel in Wasilla. It was all very exciting, and I had mixed emotions. I wanted to sleep, yet at the same time I wanted to relive in my mind every moment of our race. Once we got back to the kennel we went to our houses and relaxed until dinner.

Vern, Susan and Mom were busy getting things ready for dinner. Vern always hosted a pre-race dinner for all of his friends and Lee's group from South Dakota. This time, the group included all of Mom's friends that came to Alaska for the start of the race. It was a tradition for everyone to make guesses about the winner, the rookie of the year, and several other positions. Lee would score all of the sheets and choose winners depending on what they'd picked. Lee took care of the details, and I don't think anyone truly understood how it worked but Lee was the inventor of the game and he understood the rules, so everything would be fine. We could hear a lot of laughing while people made their predictions. The people were having fun, but we were thinking about the race to come. The dog yard was quiet, restful and thoughtful, but I was still wondering what it would be like out there.

Mom left Vern's place and headed back to her quarters to go to bed early, but she told us the next morning she had a hard time sleeping. Like us, she had many thoughts floating around in her brain. Like us, she was wondering about choices we would all be making the next day.

Chapter 10

The Re-Start:

It was a beautiful day at the kennel. Mom and Glen woke up early and they ate something light. Leora was next door, and Mike was sleeping on a bed in the "great room." Misha and Vern fed all of us and packed the truck to head to the start. Susan had to take Dee Dee to the emergency room during the night because of some excruciating pain in her lower back. That gave us two less pairs of hands but everything got loaded and we were ready to go. Mom woke Mike up and we all headed to Willow to go to the staging area by 10 AM so there would be plenty of time to get things ready for the re-start.

Once there, Glen, Mike and Mom headed to the community center to have breakfast and try to relax. She said it was a wonderful and festive atmosphere with a lot of craft vendors selling their wares. Because Mom had the #3 starting position, we would leave at 2:04 PM. There were many visitors in the staging area. Louise from DogBooties.com stopped by as well as the lady that sewed my dog booties. People from Mom's church in Wasilla and her friends from South Dakota and North Dakota made it a special day. Ellen Halverson and her son Peter were also there helping. Everything was so exciting that Mom could have come apart, but for some reason she was very calm. Maybe that's why we were all so calm also. Several people commented on how nice and calm we all looked. It was so special to have Glen and Mike there as we had not seen them since Mike left for school and we left home to come to Alaska.

When it came our time to head to the start it went as smooth as silk. We got in the starting chute and Mom thanked all of the volunteers that were helping. Right before the start she got a hug and good wishes from David Monson, Susan Butcher's husband. What a special treat! Then 3-2-1 and we were off down the chute past hundreds of waving fans and friends. Keeping my feet on the ground and running was so much fun. I wanted to run even faster. But I listened to Mom and did exactly what she said.

What an exciting time! I was surprised to find out that once we headed out onto the trail we weren't alone for quite some time, unlike most of our races. The fans continued past the Yentna checkpoint all the way to Skwentna and beyond. Some people were out in various places along the trail, camping out, cooking food, and watching us run by like we were in a parade. Sometimes the food they were cooking smelled so good that I was tempted to stop for a snack, but Mom said "On By!" and I always try to listen to Mom so I went on by. I tried to remember every moment because we were doing something we'd worked so hard to do!

The run to Yentna was great and we had no problems. We were all enjoying the excitement. We were listening to everything Mom said even with all of the airplanes and snow machines on the river to distract us. It was truly exciting!

Chapter 11

Racing.. Really Racing!

We arrived in Yentna at 6:15 PM. Mom stopped and put straw down for us and then made us a great meal of Salmon and kibble. She changed our booties. We only stayed for 3 hours and then left for Skwentna.

It was a beautiful run to Skwentna, although it was warmer than we would like. When we arrived it was 1 AM. Again, Mom gave us fresh new straw and started to make our dinner. Then Mom spoke to Greg Heister from the Iditarod Insider. After a quick interview, Mom took off our booties and oiled our feet. After two hours we got to eat the Salmon meal. It was so good that I wanted seconds and thirds but no such luck. It would have made us sick to eat too much. I think it would have been worth it! After that, Mom started another meal for us and a vet came by to check each of us out. We got a smiley face in the vet book, which meant we were all doing well. After four hours, we got to eat again and then Mom headed in to rest and eat something for herself.

When Mom came back out it was too warm to put our booties on because the snow would stick to them and then ball up, possibly hurting us. So, Mom applied our foot salve very liberally to both the inside and the outside of our feet. Next, Mom had to pack the return bag and then repack the sled. When that was done, Mom got ready to leave and we pulled out at 8:30 AM. We were eager for our next run!

The trip to Finger Lake was beautiful, although it was very slow and punchy due to the warm temperatures. We arrived at 2:28 PM. As we were nearing the checkpoint, Mom heard a plane overhead, and looked up and saw that it was a red Beaver. She thought it looked like the type of plane she had flown out on the trail in before, and was hopeful that Glen and Mike would be there. To her great pleasure it turned out to be them. Mom's friends, Leora and Stacy and Diane were with them. She didn't get a chance to visit with them, but was glad to know they were there.

Mom is great about routine. She followed the same routine as at the last two checkpoints. While she was working, Mike came to tell her that some ravens had broken in to the drop bag she had sent to Rainy Pass, so he had brought her a new drop bag of dog food. Mike told Mom he was going to take it to Rainy Pass but the weather made it impossible, so he had brought it to her there. The race judge insisted that Mom carry the food with her. She didn't want to add the extra weight, so she made the choice to only take part of it. Then the vets looked at us and we got another smiley face. Mom rested in the sleeping tent, and went to the lodge for some homemade ice cream. When she came back she salved our feet again, but didn't put booties on us because the snow coming down was wet and sticky.

Chapter 12

A Beautiful Snowy Evening Turns Crazy

We left for Rainy Pass at 10 PM. It was a beautiful evening and Mom said we were moving so well and thought how wonderful it all was. Perhaps that was not a good thing to think about out loud, because eight or nine miles out of the checkpoint I suddenly heard a horrible sound. I realized that we broke the right runner completely off Mom's sled at the back stanchion. It was a real bummer, because it made it almost impossible for Mom to steer and control the sled.

The trail to Rainy Pass is some of the worst trail in the race. Needless to say, Mom tipped over and was upside down much of the time. In the darkness, we kept trying to move forward. Every left turn was a crash, and every other right turn was a crash too. Mom spent a lot of time putting the sled upright, and then there would be another crash. It was a slow process of moving forward, crashing, up righting the sled, moving forward, crashing, up righting the sled, and forward again until the next turn and the next crash. It seemed endless and we all felt a sadness and desperation as we knew something was terribly wrong because Mom never drove the sled this way.

Suddenly, WHAM! It couldn't have gotten worse, but it did.

We came to an immediate stop. There was no more forward movement. No more crashing and up-righting, only a solid stop. Frozen in the darkness, I blinked through the dark and tried to shake off the jolt, only to realize we had been in a huge crash in the first portion of the famous steps and the sled had gone sailing off to the right side of the trail and slammed into a tree.

Mom tried to no avail to upright the sled. She tried again, and we even tried to help by pulling, but we were not successful. We weren't alone on the trail, and Mom was worried about other mushers who were coming up behind us and that we would cause them to crash. Or worse, they would crash into us. This was a time for thinking carefully and clearly, for using our problem solving skills. She figured the safest thing to do would be to get us dogs off of the trail so she tied us to any tree or any piece of brush she could find. Needless to say, she was pretty tired and sore from hours of hitting the ground. We hadn't seen her do anything like this before, and we all thought she had lost her mind to tie us to trees on the side of the hill, so none of us were having much fun at this time. I'll admit, there was a little bit of grumbling going on from us, and a little feeling of desperation as we were being tied to trees. We wanted to move forward and understand this cruel event. The fear of what might happen next kept us all unsettled.

Soon, a very nice musher passed. He suggested to Mom to take the gang line off the sled, put us back on it, and he would tie us up at the bottom of the steps on the Happy River. Mom tried to do this, but it didn't work, because we wouldn't leave. We just tied ourselves up into a ball. We were a team, and it didn't seem right for us to leave the sled like that. We were restless and concerned because of what we were being asked to do in the cold darkness of this unfamiliar trail. Mom was retying us back to the trees when another team came by and then wrecked because we accidentally spooked the musher's dogs. Mom felt terrible about that. Mom tried to warn the next few approaching teams but it was hard as she really needed to attend to us at the same time. Two more mushers arrived next, and both stopped to help Mom. One of them helped Mom get her sled back on the trail. One of them bent a runner going down the next step so he was busy with his own issues. This was an exhausting experience and I found myself thinking about my house back at Vern's kennel, and even about my house back in North Dakota.

Once the sled was back on the trail, Mom continued working to get us moving again. She attached most of us back to the sled, but only with neck lines. She didn't hook all of us up, because she didn't want all of the power even though we only had neck lines attached. There was another big vertical before us which meant the possibility of another big crash.

Once down the next step, Mom hooked the team down and made sure they were tied off the trail. Mom came back to get the dogs she'd left. She thought we would all follow, so she turned us loose. We do this all the time at the kennel, so she didn't think it would be a problem. Everyone except for me, Nigel, fell into step with Mom and did just what she said. I got spooked and I ran off the trail. I knew where they were all going, but I just couldn't follow them. Maybe I could later, but not right then.

I watched through the darkness. After attaching the

dogs that followed to the gang line, Mom returned to get me. She knows I like snacks, so she brought me some very tempting food. I was tempted, but I didn't want to come, so Mom went back to the sled. I knew Mom was disappointed in me. I was confused. It was so odd that Mom had tied us to the trees off on a steep ledge the way she did. I watched as Mom worked fixing a meal for the rest of the dogs. The other two mushers were busy getting the sled with the bent runner ready to go. One of the mushers started cutting wood for a fire for mom. She wanted to change her clothes because she'd been sweating and was wet. She also wanted to rest for a few minutes. Mom felt confident that after she rested for awhile she'd be able to get me and continue moving forward even though the sled was broken. There was some discussion and Mom told them to go on with their races. One of the mushers wanted to be overly helpful, and decided to help her by going after me. Mom told him it was a mistake, but he went anyway. He scared me so much that off I went, as fast as I could to find a safe place and hopefully some interesting food. I didn't see Mom after that for a long time until she rescued me with a plane at Tala Vista Lodge.

I could tell that Mom was very frustrated because before I had been chased I was sitting at the top of the step looking at what was going on. Mom truly appreciated the help and concern, but at some point she just wanted to get things done herself and not be told what she should do. Mom knew the race rules, and what would happen to her if she arrived without a team member. Her helpers finally left and gave her part of their Heet. Mom did use it on the way to Rainy Pass and was glad that they left it.

In the darkness, still frightened, I watched Mom and

the team. After changing her clothes, she fed the dogs and laid on the sled to rest. She called me on and off and rested a little longer. Then, she took some aspirin and laid on the sled to rest again. She fell asleep and I watched her.

She woke up and then gave the dogs a nice kibble and water soup before she tried to get underway again. Several times she called out to me, and I watched her. I heard her, but I was too spooked and needed time. Not too long before she was ready to leave another musher came by. He checked to see if Mom was OK, and she assured him she was. He said another musher was coming and if she didn't mind she could wait for her on the river. Mom said she would, and he left. Mom only had neck lines hooked as she went down to the river. She went down a little way so that the other musher had room, and hooked the team down. She put all their tugs on and finished just as the other musher arrived. They greeted each other and then continued. Again, it was difficult for Mom to steer and control the sled. Right turns were doable some of the time, but left turns were near impossible. The trail consisted of one right turn, then one left turn. Needless to say Mom was on the ground a good amount of the time.

Before long, Mom and my teammates were out of sight. I was again tempted to follow them but could not bring myself to do it. I was just too confused about what was happening. I've listened to stories of what happened next. Here is what I know.

After a few hours, she had the sled upside down again to the point that she could not move it. She waited for the other musher to catch up, and she helped her get it up and off another tree. She hooked the team down and then helped the other musher get her team by.

Then she fed our team and rested so she could continue. Mom blanketed all of the dogs as they were on an icy trail and she wanted them to be as warm as possible. I think they were only 6 miles from Rainy Pass which, under good sled conditions is only 40 or 50 minutes. But with a broken sled runner, it took hours.

She finally got going again after resting and cooking for the dogs and herself. She had some beef Stroganoff and some pine needle water. Mom couldn't find snow that didn't have pine needles in it, so she was stuck fixing herself and us a very tasty new flavored water. Since the snow was boiled it was pretty safe to drink, and it was important for Mom to stay hydrated as well. She traveled a few miles and ran into a group of snow machines. They asked Mom if she had seen the lady who had only one runner and she said "That would be me." They asked if she was OK and if she wanted some water. Mom was happy to take vitamin water and thanked them. They wanted to know how to help and Mom asked them to stay far enough behind to not scare the dogs. They were so kind and nice and did exactly as she asked. Mom finally arrived at Rainy Pass, having been upside down a few more times, at 10:02 PM, 24 hours after she left Finger Lake. What a miserable run and a disappointment to have a broken sled and have a missing dog.

Chapter 13

The Unthinkable - To Scratch

Mom hooked the team down, gave them some straw and a snack, and then answered some questions from the Anchorage Daily News reporters and their camera man. They asked Mom if she remembered that in 2007 Lance Mackey had lost a runner in the same area. She said she had and wished she had his youth and agility. The vets arrived to look at the other dogs and the race officials arrived and spoke to Mom. She told them that she would have to scratch because she didn't have all of her team members and her sled was destroyed. I was the one who was not with her, of course, and now I feel really terrible about that. The race volunteers brought Mom the paperwork later and she signed it; officially scratching.

Mom was very devastated to have her race end this way. She was more upset though that I, Nigel, was lost. She went into the checkpoint and they asked her to come to the lodge for dinner. Mom had corn and ham and great company to visit with as she ate. There was bread and juice and anything else you could want. The lodge owners Denise and Steve Perrin were very gracious and kind to her. The camera man from the Anchorage Daily News let Mom use his computer to email Glen about the situation. Mom left the lodge and headed towards her team. As she was walking to the team she was invited to stay in the COMMS area of the checkpoint by one of the race volunteers. They put up a cot for her and after mom returned from checking the team she tried to go to sleep.

I don't think she slept very well, but she said she did get some sleep. I didn't get much either. When Mom woke up in the morning, she started breakfast for all the dogs, except me. I was on my way back to Vern's. I'd have to find my own breakfast, my own lunch and snacks, and my own way back to the re-start area. That was my goal.

Mom went to the lodge for breakfast and visited with some of the guests there. She was told she would be flown out as soon as a flight could land on the lake. After breakfast Mom went back to check on the dogs. She made them some thin soup and was pleased they drank it all. Ellen, one of Vern's dogs that ran with the team was having a hard time resting so Mom sat down with her and she finally laid down. They both fell asleep on the nice hay. They use hay at Rainy Pass because the Perrin's have horses that can eat the hay after the dogs sleep on it. It is a nice way not to waste anything.

There was a lady staying at the lodge who was flying an ultra-light up the trail. The ceiling was too low to fly over the pass and continue her journey, so she was giving rides to anyone who wanted one. They seemed to be enjoying themselves but Mom was not interested because she doesn't like heights. And, in her heart, she was thinking about the end of her race and me, wondering where I had gone.

Mom also met a very nice guest named Susan, and she visited with her quite some time. Susan from Richmond Virginia is also a painter like Mom. They spent time talking about watercolor and many other things. As sad as Mom was, it helped to have such nice, kind people around her. She kept hoping she would hear something about me, Nigel, but no reports came in until later that day or the next day. She heard some snow machine drivers had seen a white dog in the area of the Happy River. Vicki, the ultra-light pilot offered to fly Mom down the trail to look for me.

Mom fed the dogs dinner and then had another wonderful meal at the lodge. They were having a get together after dinner but Mom opted to go to bed as she was tired and sore. She went right to sleep but woke at 3 AM. She was too sore to stay in bed so she got up and went to start breakfast for the dogs. At 3:30 AM a herd of horses started across the dog yard on the lake. The night before, the horses were in a pen at the top of the hill so Mom went to wake Steve to make sure they should be loose. She felt bad getting him up at 3:40 AM, but she did not want anything to happen to the horses if they shouldn't be out. He thanked Mom and said it was OK for them to be there. Mom returned, fed the dogs, and then went back to the check point COMMS building.

Mom joined everyone in the lodge for breakfast. Vicki offered again to take her up in her ultra-light to look for me. Mom finally agreed so she went back to her sled to put on her heavy clothes. Making this choice to fly with Vicki was not an easy thing to do. Mom had a fear of heights in something like this ultra light. I knew she must really love me and want me found if she were to put her fears behind her and climb into that craft! I was so proud of her when I heard the story! That's my Mom!

The race staff said she had quite a bit of time to do this because the drop dogs would fly out first, then her dogs. Then, her equipment would be flown out, and then she would be flown last. So, she agreed to fly with Vicki. After putting on her heavy clothes she got into the ultra-light with Vicki in front of her. They took off and headed down the trail toward Finger Lake. They circled several times to make sure that tracks they saw coming down the river were not mine. They landed at Finger Lake and spoke to the lodge owner, Carl.

Then they took off again to return down the trail. They saw two dog teams just before the steps and decided to land by the Happy River to see if they had seen anything. After they landed Mom walked down the trail and Vicki stomped a path so they could turn the ultra-light around.

Mom met the dog teams and found GB Jones on the second sled. He was headed to Rainy Pass Lodge to pick up a few items he left two years ago when he lost a dog in that area. He reassured Mom she would find me, after all, his dog was found when this happened to him. Then he headed off down the trail.

When Mom finally returned to Rainy Pass she found that her team had just left for Anchorage. She needed to break down her sled so it could go next and then she would leave after all of her equipment did. Mom spoke to Carl, the care taker at Rainy Pass, to see if she could borrow some tools. He told Mom he would met her at her sled to see what she needed. When he arrived they looked at the sled to decide what to do. He said he would break it down and loaded it in a toboggan to take to his shop. When he returned it was in three pieces and all of the small parts were in a can so Mom would not lose them. When they loaded it into the plane the pilot said it was the best broken down sled to load that he had ever had. Mom shared that information with Carl and thanked him for helping her. Once all of Mom's gear was loaded, the plane left again and headed to Anchorage. That meant the next plane that came was for Mom to fly out of Rainy Pass. It came very soon after her gear left. Sharon, Carl's wife and Mom got on board. The pilot was Wes, who flies air cargo. He said when he'd heard Mom was up in an ultra-light he said a prayer for her. Sharon was heading to Anchorage so she could go to work at White Mountain during the race. White Mountain is the next to last check point on the trail. The mushers must stay there for eight hours, so there is a lot of work to do. It is amazing how many people are needed to pull off this race, and how they must all work together all along the Iditarod Trail for the race to be successful.

As Mom left Rainy Pass, her thoughts were jumbled. She was very sad I was not with her and her race had ended. She knew there were so many family and friends who were disappointed that she did not finish. She felt like she had let down her sponsors and also Vern and Susan. At the same time she was amazed how kind everyone was to her at Rainy Pass and was pleased she had met so many nice people. Most of all she was just worried about me and hoped I was OK and she would find me soon.

Once back in Anchorage, Mom met Misha and Dee Dee who had all the dogs loaded into the truck already. They were in the Millennium Hotel in Anchorage, the offical race Headquarters during the race, so Mom decided to join them. Mom's friend Diane Johnson came over and greeted her, and her friend Mark Kellerher from Logistics, an Iditarod friend for several years, was there for a supporting hug. Mom received many kinds words of encouragement that I would be found. There were many tears shed before she finally left with Misha and Dee Dee. Misha drove because Mom was just too sore and tired. It was nice for her to get back to the kennel and the dogs were happy to be home. I think Mom was glad to be back but very sad with the circumstances, and very sad that I wasn't with her and the rest of the team.

Chapter 14

Mommy-Choosing My Way

Back at the kennel that evening, Mom went to bed and awoke in the morning with the mission to find out where to begin looking for me. Vern suggested Mom call Finger Lake and then Denali Flight Service in Willow. Mom called Carl at Winter Lake Lodge to see if he had a snow machine that she could rent or borrow. He did not but suggested Mom call his neighbor Joe Beach. Mom then called Denali Flight Service to see if Barry Stanley could fly her out on the trail. When Mom called Denali Flight Service, Barry was not there. The lady who answered asked Mom what she needed and Mom mentioned she wanted to find out about flying to Finger Lake and maybe Joe Beach's place so she could look for me. The lady on the other end said Joe Beach was there, and would she like to talk to him. What an amazing turn. Mom spoke to Joe and he said he had just come in by snow machine. He said as he traveled south on the Skwentna River he saw some tracks that were too big for a coyote and too small for a wolf. He figured it was a 60 pound sled dog. He thought the dog was stopping at all of the camp sites to forage for snacks and then moving on down the trail. He said the dog was probably past the Skwentna checkpoint heading toward Shell Lake. Mom thanked him and immediately called Iditarod Logistics.

Mom's friend Mark answered and she shared the information. He said "We're on it." He called Mom back about

15 minutes later and told her to go to Willow Air by the gas pump as he was sending a plane for her. Mom also spoke to her friend Diane Johnson and she shared that someone had called about Nigel near Skwentna. When she got to the gas pump she called Mark to let him know she was there. He asked her what the ceiling looked like and she shared it was snowing. He said that she needed to go to Big Lake airport. Mark gave Mom directions on how to find Big Lake Air and she immediately headed out in that direction. She arrived just as Phil Morgan, with the Iditarod Air Force arrived.

They both used the facility and then headed for the Skwentna Checkpoint. They circled and tried to land on the river because Phil was told to try and land there by the Iditarod Logistics team. They even skimmed the river but Phil decided they needed to land at the airstrip across the river from the checkpoint. As soon as they landed they were greeted by the postmaster, Joe Dahlia and his beagle, Mac. They were both on Joe's snow machine. Joe and Mac took Mom to the checkpoint. At the checkpoint, Norma, Joe's wife told her they'd heard a dog was found at the old Skwentna checkpoint. Mom returned to the plane and talked to Phil about heading for the old Skwentna Lodge. Phil had never been there but thought he knew where it was. They began to circle and Phil said he thought the lodge was just below them. Mom saw two snow machines on the river, and thought she saw a landing strip next to them. Phil said that they would go to investigate it and prepared to land on the river. After landing, and as they approached the snow machines, Mom saw me, Nigel, still wearing my neon green t-shirt, just standing there with the lodge owners as if I was in charge of the whole scene.

Phil could not stop the plane fast enough for Mom. As soon as it was stopped Mom jumped out and once I heard Mom's voice we had a very happy reunion. Mom brought me something to eat. In fact it was one of my favorite meals, beef hearts and kibble. Needless to say I finished it all. The lodge owners were wonderful. They shared with Mom that a girl named Elizabeth actually coaxed me in with food and a kind voice. The lodge is now called Talvista Lodge and it is owned by Chris, Sara, and Miranda Poynter. They were as happy as I was to be reunited with my mom.

Mom visited with them for a short time and then I headed back to the plane with her and the pilot Phil. Phil opened the cargo door and I jumped in like I flew all the time at home, and that flying was my favorite mode of transportation instead of pulling a sled. I curled up on the padded floor and went right to sleep. I started to have the most wonderful dream, right away. I dreamed that I was safe and sound with my Mom. Suddenly the sounds that scared me while I'd been on my own, the scary person who had spooked me off, and all of the sad things that happened to us seemed to drift away.

Once we landed at Big Lake, Mom and I got in her truck and then Mom returned a call from Chas St George of Iditarod. I listened in to the phone call and was so excited to hear what he said. Here I thought everyone was going to be mad at me for running off but instead, everyone was so happy Mom had found me. Then I heard some really fun news! There was going to be a press conference at the Millennium Hotel and I was going to be the star of the press conference. Me, Nigel, the star! Mom and I headed to Anchorage for my press conference. Mom received a phone call from Stan Hooley, the Executive Director of the Iditarod, to say he was happy I was safe. Keeping dogs safe is a main priority of the Iditarod and I can testify to that!

Once I arrived at the Millennium, I was received like a hero. Chas gave me a big hug and then Mom got one. Everyone there was so kind that I thought it was great to be back with my humans again. I had many pictures taken and many hugs, and then was live at 5 on KTUU TV.

I wanted to tell my story: the crash, my poor mom being banged around, how some good people tried to help us and one scary shadow that spooked me off. I wanted to tell of all of the wild animals I saw, the yummy snacks I found along the way back down the trail, and the beautiful northern lights I saw while I was all alone on the trail. But, this was my first ever press conference, so all I could do was wag my tail and smile for the camera. I enjoyed the hugs, pets, and special treats. I also gave out as many doggie kisses as I could. I thought about the choices I'd made and where it led me. A broken sled led us to many crashes and my Mom had been so brave through it all. But after making the choice to run off from my team, that meant that Mom had to stop her race to Nome.

After the interview, we returned to the kennel and I was very happy to be back with my fur friends and ready for a delicious meal. I told my dog yard buddies my whole story and they told me that while I was having an adventure of my own, they slept in hay, watched horses, saw other sights, and flew in a plane too.

That night while I waited for sleep to come I had time to think and realize that there are many lessons in this story. One should never run away from those that love and care for them. It really does cause heartache and trouble. Needless to say it caused a lot of people to go out of their way to find me, for which I am forever grateful.

For me, I just wanted to say thank you to everyone who was concerned and helped to find me. Also a big thank you to the Iditarod and its commitment to us dogs to insure that we are always number one. Without their help, I may still be looking for my Mom.

Epilogue

I guess you are wondering why my book is named Nigel's choice. Well, if you haven't figured it out, there is a chance that my Mom could have continued if she had gotten her second sled in time, and if I had not decided to head back home after being chased. My choice of getting spooked off, led to different events than we had planned and worked for. We couldn't finish the Last Great Race, Iditarod.

Our Iditarod was something different – it was a run from Anchorage to Rainy Pass. But, we all learned how our choices can affect others in ways we never thought about. It was Mom's choice and ours to start it, and it was my choice about how it ended.

From choices come actions, and from actions there are results. This is a good lesson for anyone to learn, at any age. Because, when we make choices, they have affects that we might never think of.

I guess we will never know if we could have finished that wonderful event. The choice I made kept us from finding out. But, when you think about it, Nome wasn't the most important thing, was it?

Every choice one makes leads to a result and what you do with the choices and results becomes yet another choice along your own "personal Iditarod trail."

A long and big thanks to every person who helped me along my journey. I also want to thank my Mom for her reaction after finding me. My Mom was very happy to have me home safely. I guess we are all lucky to have a Mom like that, a Mom who loves you for being you no matter what choices you make.

Happy Trials to you all, wherever they may lead you.

Nigel.

Glossary of Terms

Alaskan Sled Dog - is an unregistered very well breed mutt. Their origins go back to the Native Alaskan village dogs now mixed with some type of hound. They are breed to run and they love to do that. They are very smart dogs and come in all color variations.

Alright! - command given to start the team.

Anorak - a type of parka or jacket with a hood that usually pulls over the head. It was originally designed by Native Alaskans.

Booties - paw coverings made for the dogs to protect them from injury from sharp or rough objects. They are made of a tightly woven material which Velcro on the sled dog's feet.

Checkpoint - is a designated stopping place along a race course. It can be a village, lodge or a tent city just set up for a race.

Drop Line - is a portable cable or chain configured to attach dogs to when not on the dogsled. It can be attached between two trees or between two secure objects.

Easy! - command given to slow or relax the dog team.

Frost Boils - are up-swellings of mud that occur through the frost in permafrost areas, such as arctic and alpine regions. These can make a road very wavy when they occur as we found out when driving through the Yukon.

Gang line - is made up of 8' foot sections of braided hollow rope or cable which are put together to accommodate the number of dogs being mushed. Two dogs use one 8'section.The dogs are connected at the back by a 4' tug line and from the front by a 1' neck line both of which are attached to the gang line.

Gee! - the command to turn right.

Haw! - the command to turn left.

Heet - a car fuel tank additive used to fuel a mushers alcohol stove which they use to heat water out on the trail for the dogs and themselves.

Musher - is the name for a person who drives dogs.

Neck line - connects the dog from his collar to the gang line.

Pedaling - is when a musher stands on one runner and pushes off the ground with his other foot to assist his dog team moving forward.

Runner - is a ski like object on the bottom of the sled to allow it to move through the snow.

Runner Plastic - strips of plastic connected to the sled runner to help the sled move easier over the snow.

Sled bag - a bag fitted to the sled to hold items needed by the musher.

Snow Hook - a metal hook with claws used to secure a dog team to the snow, or other secure items, when stopped.

Snub Line - a line attached to the gang line to hold a dog team to a secure object when stopped.

Trail! - word used by a team coming on another team from behind requesting they be given the trail.

Tug line - line used to attach a dog to the gang line from behind.

Whoa! - the command used to stop the dog team.

There are many other commands used by other mushers but these are the ones I used while racing in Alaska.

NANCY'S BIO

Hi! I'm a 61 year old mother of one son, Michael, and the wife of a very busy Otolaryngologist (ENT), Glen. I live on a 33 acre hobby farm with a frequently changing number of Alaskan Huskies, and many cats. I am an Occupational Therapist by education, and worked for 17 years in spine rehabilitation and with swallowing disorders. I have raced sled dogs since 2002, thanks to my son who got us started with them 14 years ago. Spring '09 I ran the Iditarod Sled Dog Race in Alaska. I broke my sled 8 miles out of Finger Lake and my race ended at Rainy Pass. I worked communications in '06, '07, '10 and '11 and was wishing I was on the trail. The decision was made summer '10 to close our Sled Dog kennel after 14 years of fun. I will always love them, but it has just become too hard to keep it all going. I guess I am aging.

I hope you enjoy Nigel's Choice as he tells the story of our Iditarod Adventure.

Nancy

JON'S BIO

Jon Van Zyle is the illustrator of over 30 award winning children's books and adult books. His original paintings and reproductions are exhibited in galleries and museums in the U.S. as well as Europe. He is a two time veteran of the Iditarod Sled Dog Race, and their official artist since 1979. He is also a member of the Iditarod Hall of Fame.